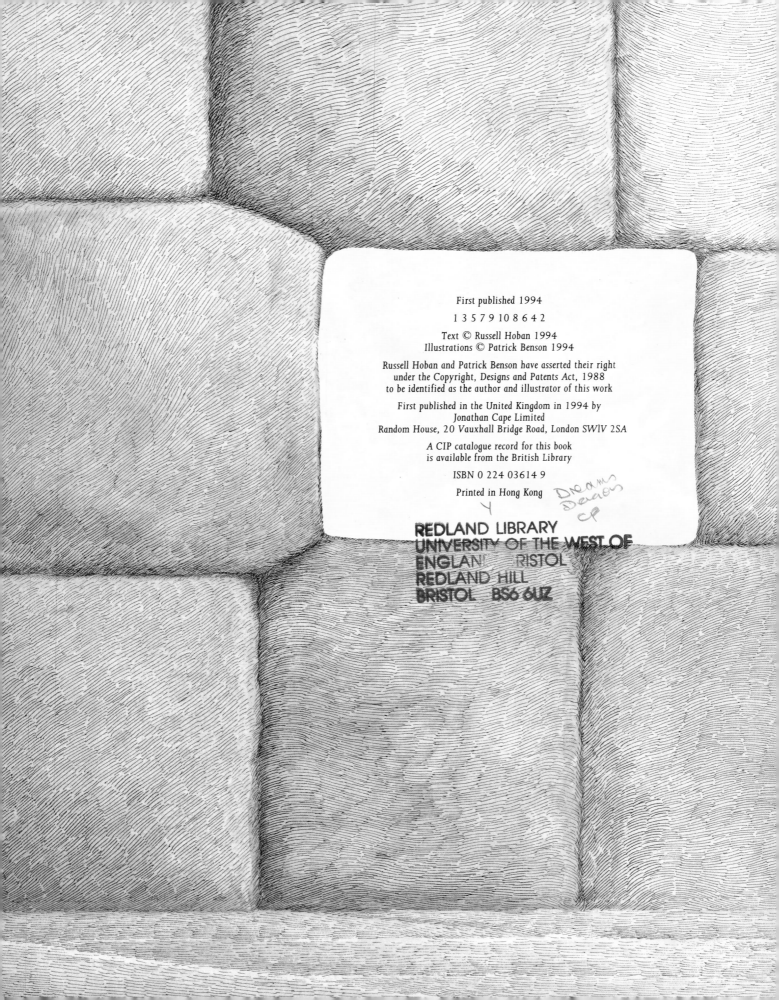

First published 1994

1 3 5 7 9 10 8 6 4 2

Text © Russell Hoban 1994
Illustrations © Patrick Benson 1994

Russell Hoban and Patrick Benson have asserted their right
under the Copyright, Designs and Patents Act, 1988
to be identified as the author and illustrator of this work

First published in the United Kingdom in 1994 by
Jonathan Cape Limited
Random House, 20 Vauxhall Bridge Road, London SWlV 2SA

A CIP catalogue record for this book
is available from the British Library

ISBN 0 224 03614 9

Printed in Hong Kong

RUSSELL HOBAN

THE COURT OF THE

WINGED
SERPENT

PATRICK BENSON

JONATHAN CAPE
London

John was dreaming. In the dream he was alone in a jungle. He heard the cries of unseen birds and animals as he struggled through heavy undergrowth. He was worried about snakes and spiders and scorpions. He heard something behind him but he didn't look back. He wondered if he would ever see home again.

He came to a muddy brown river. It was moving very fast, curving and coiling like a great brown serpent.

Now he could hear that whatever was behind him was closer than before.

An empty dugout canoe shot past and he jumped into it.

He looked back and saw something reach out of the jungle for him but he couldn't see it clearly.

Now John could see the sky, it was yellow. He didn't like the look of it.

The current was running faster, the jungle blurred past on both sides. John heard a roaring in the distance, it grew louder and louder.

Pitching and rolling in white water, the canoe sped between great black cliffs. Up ahead John saw mist and spray and sky. Far below he saw the tops of trees. The roaring was louder, it seemed to shake the sky. He was almost at the edge of a waterfall.

The canoe slammed into a wall of black rock and John leaped on to a narrow ledge.

In the cliff was a large opening made by water long ago.

Inside it John could see nothing but blackness.

On both sides of the opening the ledge narrowed away to nothing. Below was the waterfall and above was the sheer face of the cliff.

John went into the blackness. The passage was low and narrow and it went up steeply. John climbed on all fours for a long time. He could still hear the distant roar of the waterfall and he could hear water dripping from the walls of the passage. And he heard something behind him.

John climbed as fast as he could. The passage grew lighter and he came out into a courtyard under the yellow sky.

In it was a great winged serpent of stone. It was uglier than any dragon John had ever seen in pictures. Its stone eyes glared coldly at him.

The courtyard floor and walls were of large smooth white stones so closely fitted together that the point of a knife could not have gone between them. The walls were forty feet high, too smooth for climbing. Above them loomed the black mountain. Facing the passage that John had come out of was a great carved stone door. There was no other way out.

There was a noise from the passage.

John ran to the stone door but there was no handle or ring to open it with.

The carving on the door was the same winged serpent that was in the courtyard. John took hold of it and pulled but the door didn't move.

The winged serpent on the door was coiled around a small stone box. On the lid of the box was carved: YBENEXTTI MEMA. John sounded it out: 'EE-BEN-EXT-TEE ME-MA.'

He was about to open the box when he heard a footstep. He turned and saw himself. It wasn't like looking in a mirror, it was another John.

'Say something,' said John to the other John.

The other John wrote with his finger on a stone: 'I HAVE NO VOICE HERE. I AM YOUR WAKING SELF. IT'S TIME FOR YOU TO BE ME, BACK IN YOUR BED AT HOME.'
'Why can't I be me a little longer?' said John.

There was a thud behind the other John. Where the opening of the passage had been there was a solid wall of stone.
'WAKING UP IS THE ONLY WAY BACK,' wrote the other John.
'IN A MOMENT IT WILL BE TOO LATE. HURRY!'

'Hang on,' said John. 'I shan't be a moment.' He opened the stone box on the winged-serpent door and took out a large emerald shaped something like a key.

He was looking for a keyhole when a huge shadow passed over him. There was a shriek that sounded as if it came from millions of years ago.

John turned and saw the other John in the talons of a tremendous winged serpent with glittering emerald-green scales.

'*Wait!*' he shouted as the serpent leapt into the air and flew off with the other John.

Stupid thing to shout, thought John. He was sitting up in bed at home and Mum and Dad were there.

'You must have had a bad dream,' said Mum.
'It was worse for the other John,' said John.
'What other John?' said Dad.
'My waking self,' said John. 'The winged serpent's got him.'

'It's all right, dear,' said Mum. 'You're awake now.'
'No, I'm not,' said John. 'I'm the dream John. The waking John's been taken by the winged serpent. Why didn't I listen to him?'
'I'll fix you some hot cocoa,' said Mum. 'Then you can get back to sleep.'
'How can the dream John sleep?' said John. 'I've got to go back there and help the waking John.'

'What can you do?' said Dad.
'I don't know,' said John. 'But I can't leave my waking self stuck in a dream. I've got to get this sorted out.'

'Try not to think about it,' said Dad.
'You've got school tomorrow and you don't want to be all worn out.'
'School!' said John. 'How can the dream John go to school?'

'Maybe you can do it in your sleep,' said Dad.
'Here's your cocoa,' said Mum.
'Try to get some rest now.'

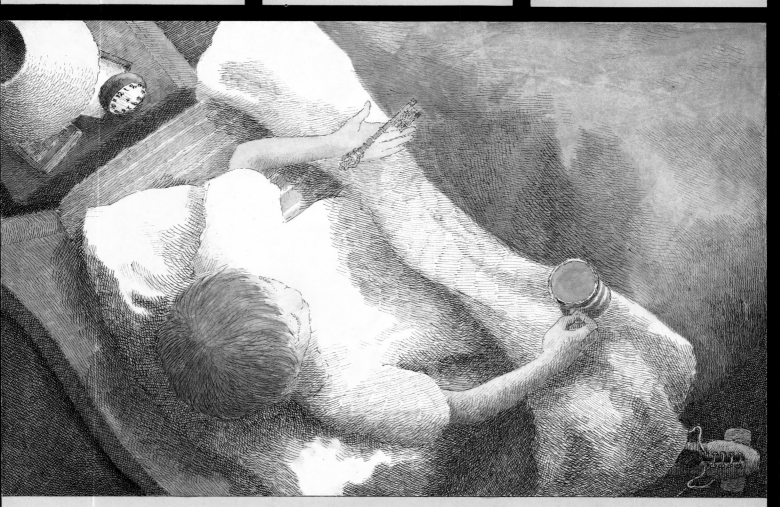

As John reached for the cocoa he saw that he was still holding the emerald key to the winged-serpent door. What was behind that door? Would he ever find out? How was he going to rescue the waking John?
There were letters cut into the key: YBENEXTTI MEMA. John stared hard as the letters became English words: MAYBE NEXT TIME.
As soon as Mum and Dad were out of the room John closed his eyes and turned the key three times. 'Ybenextti Mema,' he said.

When he opened his eyes he was in the court of the winged serpent. This time the sky was black, the mountain was purple, and the stones of the courtyard and the walls were red. The stone winged serpent in the courtyard and the one on the door were blue.

'I hope I'm not too late,' said John. He looked closely at the winged serpent on the stone door and he found the keyhole in one of its eyes.

He put the emerald key in the keyhole and turned it. The door swung smoothly open.

John stepped into blackness and the door closed behind him. The emerald key began to glow brightly. By its light John went up a long stone stairway inside the mountain. Higher and higher he climbed. He wondered when and where the stairs would end. After a long time he felt moving air on his face and he smelled a terrible stench.

John came out of the darkness at the top of the purple mountain under the black sky. He heard a horrible shrieking kind of laugh.
Crouching in front of him was the winged serpent with its emerald scales glittering in the dark light of the sky. In its talons was John's waking self.

The serpent grinned a hideous grin. 'Aaarrgghhhhh,' it said. 'I knew you'd be back, Johnny.' Its voice was hoarse and dreadful.
'You can't eat real John,' said John. 'You're just a dream.'

'But I can eat you,' said the serpent as it breathed its terrible breath on dream John, 'and once I've done that the other John will be stuck in this dream and I can eat him as well.'
'Then you'll have no one to dream you and you'll disappear,' said dream John.

'No one to dream me!' said the serpent. 'People all over the world are dreaming me right now, this very minute.'
Real John was shaking his head.
'Real John says no,' said dream John.
The serpent ground its teeth. 'Everybody dreams me!' it said. 'I'm everybody's bad dream.'

'No you're not,' said dream John. 'Real John is the last of the winged-serpent dreamers. Nobody else dreams you.'

'Yes, they do,' said the serpent. Its voice was unsteady.

'Tell the truth,' said dream John. 'When was the last time you were in a dream?'

'I can't remember,' mumbled the serpent.

'You're very old, aren't you?' said dream John. 'The world has changed since you were young. The only place you hear of winged serpents nowadays is in computer games.'

'What's a computer game?' said the serpent.

'You see what I mean?' said dream John. 'You're completely out of touch. Nobody takes winged serpents seriously anymore and nobody dreams them.'

'Except real John,' said the serpent. 'Real John dreams me.'

'He won't if you eat him,' said dream John.

'But I can still eat you,' said the serpent.

'Real John says, that if you do, he'll never dream you again,' said dream John.

The serpent closed its eyes and tears ran down its face. It set real John down on the ground and huddled itself up as small as it could. 'I won't eat anybody,' it said.

'This dream's over now,' said dream John. 'Its time for real John and me to go.'
'So soon!' said the serpent. 'When will he dream me again?'
'We'll have to wait and see,' said dream John, 'but for now it's goodbye.'

The two Johns turned and started down the long stone stairway inside the mountain.
About halfway down dream John stopped. 'Look,' he said, 'there's another stairway going off to the side. Maybe it's a short cut.'
Real John nodded and they went down the second stairway. Soon they smelled the jungle and they heard the cries of unseen birds and animals.

They came out of the mountain under a yellow sky and saw the jungle spread out before them.

They pushed though the undergrowth and there was the river,
moving very fast, curving and coiling like a great brown serpent.
'Look!' said dream John. 'There's the way home!' Real John
looked and saw his bed.

'I was just thinking about the serpent,' said dream John, 'how it looked when we left. There's still an hour or so before you have to
wake up. Do you think I could go back there for a while?'

Real John smiled. 'Yes,' he said silently, 'let's do it again,' and he climbed back into bed.
Dream John waited on the riverbank, and when an empty dugout canoe shot past he jumped into it. 'Nobody dreams them the way real John does it,' he said. 'He's the last of the winged-serpent dreamers.' And down the river he sped to the black cliffs again.